I BRAKE
FOR SKINKS

Reptiles Are My Life

story by
MEGAN McDONALD

pictures by
PAUL BRETT JOHNSON

Orchard Books · New York

An Imprint of Scholastic Inc.

SIX-SPOTTED GREEN TIGER BEETLE

STAG BEETLE

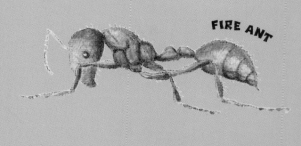
FIRE ANT

LEAF BEETLE

MOON MOTH CATERPILLAR

INSECTS:

Cool creepy crawlies with funny names like stinkbug and earwig that can run, jump, fly, hide, climb, dig, swim, and sing. Six leggers were the first creatures to fly and have been around since way before dinosaurs. Insects live everywhere— there are a billion billion of them on Earth. No lie! Everyone should go buggy for insects like I do.

—VANESSA ATALANTA

SNAKE FLY

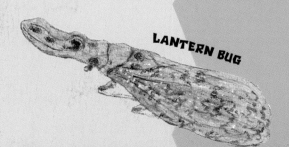
LANTERN BUG

WALKINGSTICK

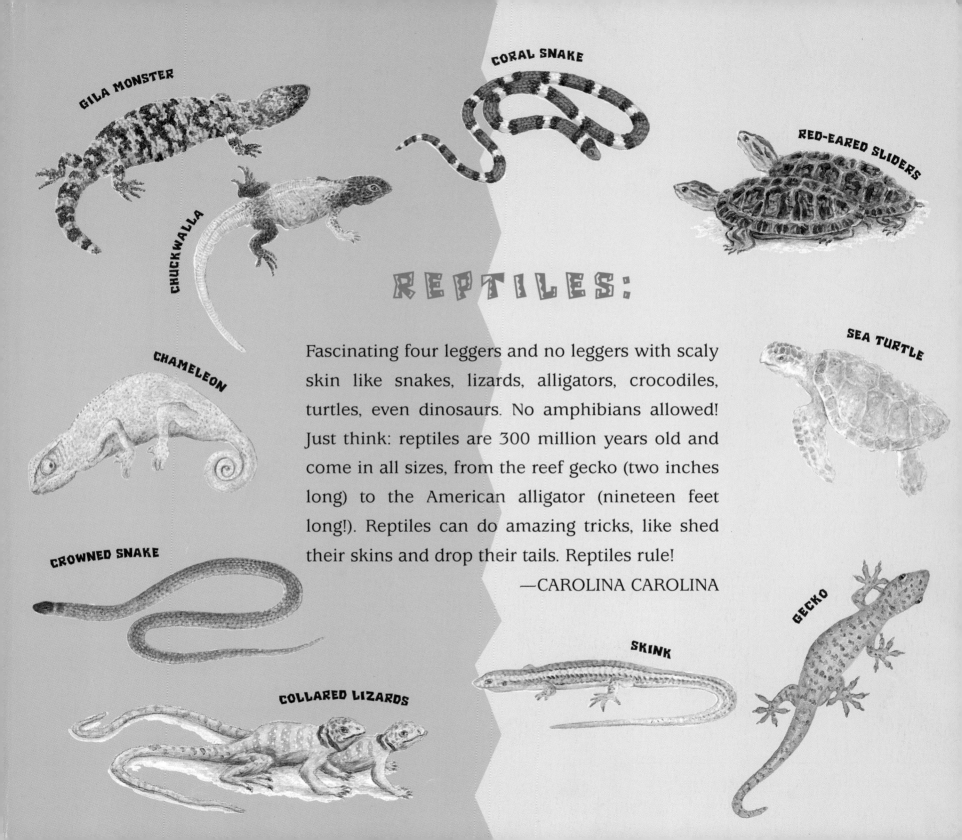

GILA MONSTER

CHUCKWALLA

CORAL SNAKE

RED-EARED SLIDERS

REPTILES:

CHAMELEON

SEA TURTLE

Fascinating four leggers and no leggers with scaly skin like snakes, lizards, alligators, crocodiles, turtles, even dinosaurs. No amphibians allowed! Just think: reptiles are 300 million years old and come in all sizes, from the reef gecko (two inches long) to the American alligator (nineteen feet long!). Reptiles can do amazing tricks, like shed their skins and drop their tails. Reptiles rule!

—CAROLINA CAROLINA

CROWNED SNAKE

SKINK

GECKO

COLLARED LIZARDS

The day Maggie poked her snake stick into a tree stump and came up with a snake fly was the day Amanda Frankenstein knew they'd be instant best friends. Forever.

Amanda was crazy about insects. Maggie was wild about reptiles.

When Amanda wore her spider Band-Aid to school, Maggie wore her rub-on tattoo of a sea turtle. The day Maggie got a fancy license plate for her bike that said I Brake for Skinks, Amanda painted her bike seat yellow, black, and red stripes—the colors of a leaf beetle. And when it came time to line up for recess, Maggie and Amanda always made up the tail.

"Whiptails!" said Maggie.

Amanda + Maggie's
Secret Rock →
KeeP AwaY!
or you will get bit by a
crocodile or a stag beetle

Maggie and Amanda were two
bugs in a rug. Two crocs on a rock.

"I'm going to change my name," Amanda told her friend at lunch.

"What's wrong with Amanda Frankenstein?" asked Maggie.

"Boring. Call me Vanessa Atalanta. It's my secret name, the scientific name for a red admiral butterfly."

"Then call me Tantilla Coronata," said Maggie. "It's scientific for the crowned snake."

"Crowned snakes give me the shivers," said Amanda. "I can't be best friends with an insect eater."

"Okay," said Maggie. "Then I will be Carolina Carolina. A box turtle."

"Do you eat insects?" asked Amanda.

"I eat worms and slugs. But mostly I eat mushrooms and berries."

"Good," said Amanda. "Have a strawberry, Carolina."

"Thank you, Vanessa," said Maggie.

In class Ms. Scorpio asked everyone to write a letter to a famous person.
Amanda took out lined paper.

Maggie used her best printing.

Dear Ms. Governor,
Please make ants the
state insect.
Yours truly,
Vanessa Atalanta
P.S. Ants are the strongest
insects in the world.

Dear Mr. President,
Please make "Alligator
Pie" the national song.
Yours truly,
Carolina Carolina
P.S. I don't eat alligators.
It's just my favorite
song.

Victor the Worm read their letters. "There's no such thing as a state bug," said Victor. "And alligator pie is green and makes you die!"

Maggie blinked. Amanda came to the rescue. "Victor, you are the spit of a spittlebug," she said. "You are the dung ball of a dung beetle."

The very next day at school, something happened. Amanda was examining a hairy caterpillar that Maggie held on her pencil. "I think it's a moon moth caterpillar," said Amanda.

"Is it really from the moon?" asked Victor.

"You're from the moon, Victor." Amanda laughed. But Maggie did not laugh with her. Maggie had her eyes on the door. Maggie was looking at the new girl.

"Meet Emily Elligator," said Ms. Scorpio.

"Alligator!" said Maggie. She dropped the moon moth caterpillar and asked if she could sharpen her pencil. She wanted to get a better look at the alligator girl, who was wearing, of all things, a gecko shirt.

"I have a gecko named Hootie," Maggie told her.

"I have a gecko named Handsome," said the new girl.

"I have a walkingstick named Slim," said Amanda. But nobody heard.

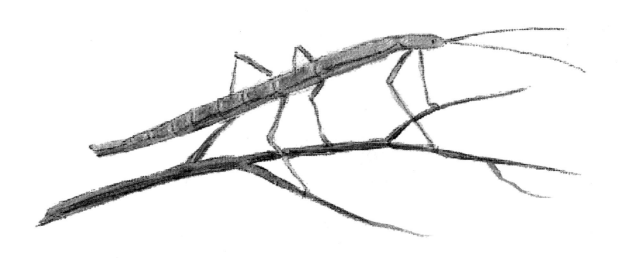

At recess Maggie was so excited about geckos, she ran to get in line next to Emily. "What about whiptails?" cried Amanda. From the back of the line, she heard Maggie say, "Reptiles are my life!"

Jiminy Cricket! Maggie had changed friends as fast as a chameleon changes colors.

On the playground Maggie and Emily chirped and barked like lizards. "Geck-oh, geck-oh, click, click!" they yelled. "We are the Gecko Girls!"

"Click, click!" yelled Amanda like a click beetle.

"That's not right!" said Emily. Maggie would not look at Amanda. She
dug the toe of her shoe into the dirt as if she were a gopher tortoise.

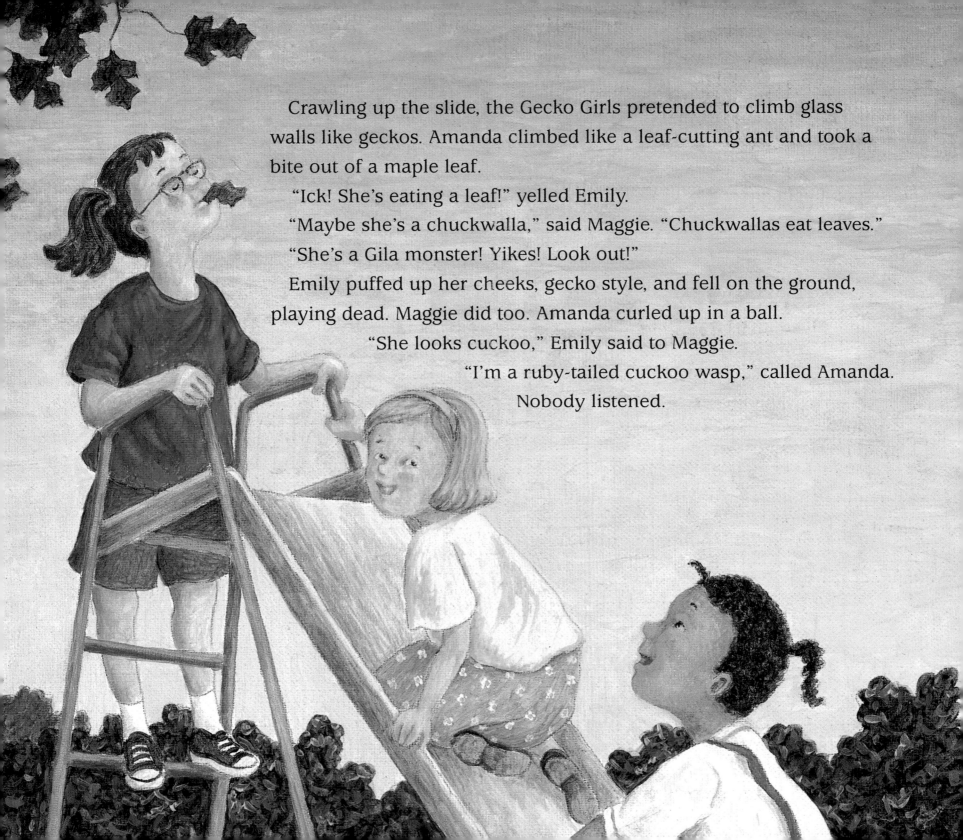

Crawling up the slide, the Gecko Girls pretended to climb glass walls like geckos. Amanda climbed like a leaf-cutting ant and took a bite out of a maple leaf.

"Ick! She's eating a leaf!" yelled Emily.

"Maybe she's a chuckwalla," said Maggie. "Chuckwallas eat leaves."

"She's a Gila monster! Yikes! Look out!"

Emily puffed up her cheeks, gecko style, and fell on the ground, playing dead. Maggie did too. Amanda curled up in a ball.

"She looks cuckoo," Emily said to Maggie.

"I'm a ruby-tailed cuckoo wasp," called Amanda.

Nobody listened.

"Handsome dropped his tail last night!" Emily told Maggie.

"Hootie dropped his tail last night too!" Maggie told Emily.

"Slim grew back a leg!" said Amanda.

Still, nobody listened.

"Everybody knows insects are for eating," said Emily.

"Everybody knows reptiles are cold-blooded," said Amanda.

If she were a stag beetle, she'd give those Gecko Girls a good pinch.

Riding bikes home, Emily and Maggie got way ahead. "See you later, alligator!" they said.

"Carolina Carolina! Wait up!" called Amanda. Nobody waited. Maggie did not even remember their secret names. Amanda felt like a louse. If only she had a friend, or two. Three louses were better than one. Three louses made lice!

Maggie and Emily were as together as two bog turtles on a log. When Emily came to school with red lipstick behind her ears, Maggie wore some too. "We're red-eared sliders!" they hissed. When the lipstick wore off, they drew two black lines around their necks and gave each other a "third eye." "Collared lizards!" they shouted.

The next day, the two
were dressed exactly alike,
in yellow, black, and red stripes.

"What's yellow, black, and red all
over?" they asked Amanda.

"Yellow, black, and read all over? The
phone book?" said Amanda.

"No! A coral snake!" said Emily.

"And a scarlet king snake!" said Maggie.

"See, we're copycats . . . different snakes,
but we look alike," said Maggie.

"We're the Snake Sisters!" said Emily.

If Amanda were a fire ant, she'd give those
Snake Sisters a good sting.

In the gym Maggie and Emily did lizard push-ups.
They scooted across the floor. "Hey, Frog Face!"
called Victor, chasing after Maggie, then Emily.
"Ribbet! Ribbet!"

"Frogs are not reptiles!" said Maggie. "They're
amphibians."

The Snake Sisters slid over the floor like
sidewinders. "I'm telling!" called Victor, looking for
Ms. Scorpio. "They stuck out their tongues at me!"

"Maggie? Emily? Is there a problem?" asked
Ms. Scorpio.

Maggie blinked. Emily blinked. Maggie's ear twitched. Emily's lip started to quiver.

Amanda Frankenstein came to the rescue. "They're the Snake Sisters. Snakes smell with their tongues," Amanda said.

"Victor. Girls," Ms. Scorpio said. "Let's stay out of smelling range."

"Thanks, Amanda," whispered Emily.

"Thanks, Vanessa Atalanta," whispered Maggie.

That afternoon they rode bikes like the wind, all three of them, fast as six-spotted green tiger beetles, fast as six-lined race runners. Amanda told her friends about the famous lantern bug that looks just like an alligator. "We are the Flying Alligators!" they screamed.

"Hey, Amanda? What's yellow, black, and red all over?" asked Emily.

"A scarlet king snake?" asked Amanda.

"No, a leaf beetle!" said Maggie.

From that day on, they were as together as three bugs in a rug, three crocs on a rock.

FOR THE WRITERS AT
BRIGHTON TOWNSHIP ELEMENTARY SCHOOL

—M.M.

All rights reserved. Published by Orchard Books, an imprint of Scholastic Inc., *Publishers since 1920.*
SCHOLASTIC, ORCHARD BOOKS, and associated logos and trademarks and/or registered trademarks of Scholastic Inc.

Library of Congress Cataloging-in-Publication Data is available upon request.

ISBN 0-439-29306-5   LC 2001016297

10 9 8 7 6 5 4 3 2 1   01 02 03 04 05

Printed in Mexico   49
First edition, August 2001

Book design by Kristina Albertson
The text of this book is set in 15 point Usherwood Medium.
The illustrations are acrylic.